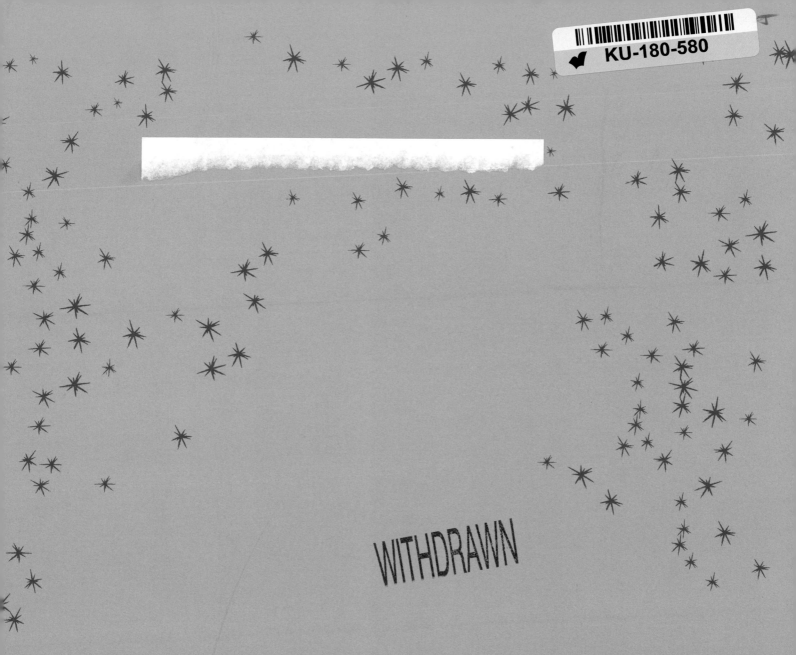

WITHDRAWN

PETER PAN AND WENDY

Hodder
Children's
Books

A division of Hachette Children's Books

PETER PAN AND WENDY
J M BARRIE
retold by May Byron for boys and girls with the approval of the author
Illustrated by Shirley Hughes

First published in Great Britain in 1925 by Hodder and Stoughton Ltd
This edition published in 2007

2

A catalogue record for this book is available from the British Library

ISBN: 978 0 340 94530 8

Printed and bound in China

The paper used in this book is a natural recyclable product made from wood grown in sustainable forests.
The hard coverboard is recycled.

Hodder Children's Books
a division of Hachette Children's Books
338 Euston Road, London NW1 3BH
An Hachette Livre UK Company

Peter Pan
and
Wendy

J M BARRIE

Illustrated by Shirley Hughes

Illustrator's foreword

When J M Barrie's *Peter Pan* was first performed in London in 1904 a reviewer predicted that 'all the world and his wife will go and see it and take their children.' He was right. It was a smash hit from the start.

I was taken to see it as a child in the 1930s and, although I never actually believed in fairies, I clapped as hard as anyone to keep Tinker Bell alive. Fairies certainly were a major feature of picture books of my childhood. In this era the traditional, sometimes sinister, nature of 'the little people' in folk tales had been carefully watered down and sentimentalised. They were depicted by illustrators like Cicily Mary Barker and Margaret Tarrant, in soft pastel colours as sweetly idealised children with wings.

It was Arthur Rackham's illustrations for Barrie's *Peter Pan in Kensington Gardens* which came closest to the somewhat unpredictable, un-nerving, creatures of the author's imagination. At the age of about nine I was given a luxurious giftbook edition with line drawings and tipped-in colour plates covered with tissue paper. Stunningly drawn and painted in low key sepia colour, these fairies flitted ravishingly through the book in the company of gnomes and elves whose faces and hands were as gnarled as the tree roots they inhabited.

Peter Pan himself appears in this story as an infant escaping from his London nursery. He flies out of the window and is for ever locked out. It is in the play *Peter Pan* and in May Byron's subsequent re-telling in the book *Peter Pan and Wendy* that his character fully emerges; the brave, wilful, maverick boy who refuses to grow up. It is a story which contains all the irresistible elements: flying, a magic island, a secret house underground and lots of fighting. Also, of course, one of the most vividly characterised pirates in children's fiction, Captain Hook. I knew exactly what he looked like when I came to draw him, that lean, suave English gent gone to the bad, with his seedy finery and terrifying hook.

Barrie created Peter Pan for the Llwellyn Davies boys, whom he adored, in the last glow of the Edwardian era. Many of their generation were destined to be the real life 'lost boys' who were killed as young servicemen fighting in World War One. But Peter Pan lives on in a story which for me, as an illustrator, presents a wonderful challenge, one in which so many remembered images come into focus.

Shirley Hughes

Contents

Chapter One

A Strange Appearance

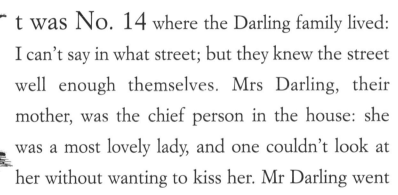It was No. 14 where the Darling family lived: I can't say in what street; but they knew the street well enough themselves. Mrs Darling, their mother, was the chief person in the house: she was a most lovely lady, and one couldn't look at her without wanting to kiss her. Mr Darling went every day to the City: and what he did there, nobody quite understood, but it was something very important. The three children were Wendy, who was nine; John, who was seven, and Michael, who was only four but tried to keep his age a secret.

Mrs Darling had two servants. Liza was the housekeeper, such a tiny little midget! – and Nana, the children's nurse, was a big Newfoundland dog. It is very uncommon, of course, to have a dog for a nurse: but Nana was a treasure. She was so fond of children that she could be trusted to look after them in every way – bath, clean clothes,

never could come back or grow up. He was supposed to live with the fairies in Kensington Gardens (which is a leafy part of London). She felt sure he was only a story, not a real child. But when she explained to Wendy, 'My love, you must have been dreaming,' Wendy said, 'Oh no, he isn't a dream. He comes through the window in the night, you see, and sits on the end of my bed, and plays to me on his pipes. It's perfectly sweet. So's he.'

'Oh, but that's nonsense!' said Mrs Darling. 'How could anybody get in? The window is three floors up.'

'Well, you see those leaves on the floor, Mother. He left them there last night. They were not there when we went to bed.'

Mrs Darling was so surprised, she could not tell what to say. Certainly there were some strange skeleton leaves on the nursery floor, by the window, and they were not off any English tree that she had ever seen. She peered about on the floor for footmarks, and she felt up the chimney with the poker. Not a sign of anybody. And it was thirty feet from the window to the pavement. Very odd.

When she talked to Mr Darling about it, he put all the blame upon Nana. He said: 'It's just the sort of rubbish a dog would stuff into children's heads. Don't take any notice.' (To tell the truth, Mr Darling and Nana did not get on very well together.) 'The children will soon forget about it if you say no more.'

But, the very next night, Mrs Darling found out for herself.

She sat beside the nursery fire, by the glimmer of three nightlights, sewing something for Michael; and she fell asleep over her work. And she dreamed that she saw the Neverland, all in a misty haze, quite close. A boy broke through the mist, leaving a gap behind him: and there were the faces of Wendy, John, and Michael gazing at her through the gap. While the dream was still there, the nursery window flew open, and a boy dropped in upon the floor. A queer little light came with him, which darted and danced about the room like quicksilver.

Mrs Darling awoke, and saw this boy – a most beautiful person about Wendy's age, dressed in skeleton leaves from unknown trees. And she was quite certain, that direct moment, that this was Peter Pan.

Chapter Two

Nana in Trouble

Mrs Darling was so startled that she screamed: and Nana, who had been for her evening out, came suddenly in through the door. Nana growled and sprang at the boy, but he disappeared through the window, which she slammed after him. Mrs Darling rushed downstairs in great distress – she was sure he must be lying killed in the street. But he was nowhere to be found. All she could see was what looked like a star shooting across the darkness.

When she got back to the nursery, Nana was holding something dark in her mouth: the something was the boy's shadow, which had been too late to escape after him. It was quite the usual sort of shadow: nothing remarkable about it. Nana wanted to hang it out of the window, in case the boy should come back to get it: but Mrs Darling thought she had better roll it up and keep it in a drawer for now, to show her husband later on. So the shadow was put away.

And nothing at all happened for a whole week. Then too many things happened much too fast – as you will see. They often do, when one least expects. It is a great bother.

A week later, on a Friday evening, Mr and Mrs Darling were dressing to go out to dinner with friends: and Nana was to be left in charge of the children. Nana was so good and faithful, and knew exactly what to do on all occasions: Mrs Darling felt that Wendy, John and Michael could not come to any harm with so kind a nurse. Nana, directly the clock struck six, got ready to give Michael his bath: when the water was on, she carried him to it on her back.

Michael was very much annoyed. He said it wasn't six o'clock yet: and that he wouldn't be bathed, and he wouldn't go to bed, and he shouldn't love Nana any more. You know the sort of bedtime won'ts that everyone says sooner or later.

Nana had heard this so many other evenings that she took no notice. She went on doing her duty as if she were deaf: and just then Mrs Darling came in, all so pretty in her white evening gown. Wendy and John, who were playing at being Father and Mother, stopped playing to look at her: and Michael jumped out of his bath in a hurry, lest she should perhaps not notice him there.

At this moment Mr Darling rushed in, frightfully excited, waving his evening tie. He was a very clever man at most things: but when it came to tying a tie, he was as weak as water-gruel. And to know this (for he did know it) made him very angry. He was very angry now. He said that unless his tie could be properly fixed he wouldn't go out to dinner, nor ever again to the office: and then they should all starve – and a great deal more. Indeed, he hardly knew what he was saying.

However, Mrs Darling tied his tie for him, quietly and quickly. And he recovered his temper at once.

He hoisted Michael on his back, and next minute they were all romping wildly round the room – Mr and Mrs Darling in their nice evening clothes, and the children in their nighties and pyjamas.

Unfortunately, just when the fun was at its jolliest, Nana accidentally rubbed up against Mr Darling as she passed, leaving long hairs all over his black dress-trousers. This upset Mr Darling again, and while Mrs Darling was brushing him, he repeated (what he had said so often that they knew it by heart) what a great mistake it was to have a dog for a nurse. It was no use telling him what a treasure Nana was: he knew all *that* by heart. But Mrs Darling could not forget how pluckily the noble animal had flown at the strange boy, and had seized his shadow. So she thought this was a good opportunity to show Mr Darling the shadow. It might soften his heart towards Nana.

Mr Darling, as you may suppose, did not know what to make of the shadow. He said, 'It isn't anybody I know: but I don't like the look of him at all.' And he thought very deeply. He was still considering when Nana entered the nursery again, carrying Michael's cough-medicine bottle in her mouth. She filled the spoon and held it out to Michael: but he was naughty and said, 'I won't! I won't!' and made faces.

His father said, 'The medicine I take is much nastier than yours, Michael, but I never make a fuss. I take it like a man.' Then Wendy had a bright idea, and fetched her father's medicine bottle, so that he could set a good example to Michael. It was nasty, sweet, sticky stuff, the colour of milk. Mr Darling simply hated it. In fact, he had hidden it away where he hoped it would never be found. He tried now to get out of having any: but when his children called him a cowardy custard, he had to pretend to take it. Wendy counted one, two, three – and Michael swallowed his spoonful manfully: but Mr Darling put his behind his back.

Of course he was seen doing this: and the children were really shocked, it was so unfair. But they were still more shocked when he poured his medicine into Nana's bowl, and told her he had put some

milk there for her. He made out that this was done for a joke: but everybody else thought it very unfunny. Poor Nana lapped up some of the milky-looking stuff – then she looked at her master with sorrowful eyes, and crawled dismally into her kennel.

Mr Darling roared with laughter, but the others wanted to cry. And he suddenly became angry for the fourth time that evening, and declared he wouldn't have that dog in the nursery for an hour longer. 'The yard,' said he, 'is the proper place for dogs.' And in spite of all Mrs Darling's entreaties and the children's tears, he enticed Nana out of her kennel, dragged her roughly away, and tied her up in the backyard. There she barked most miserably. She had never been treated like that before.

Mrs Darling, sad and silent, had to put the three little ones to bed and light their nightlights. Wendy said to her, 'The way Nana is barking now, is the way she barks when she can smell danger.'

The word 'danger' frightened Mrs Darling. Yet there did not seem to be any danger. She took care to see that the window was fastened: she sang a soft little lullaby-song over each bed; then she crept out of the nursery and joined Mr Darling, who was sitting unhappily in the passage. They picked their way across the new-fallen snow to No. 27, where they were to spend the evening. Neither of them felt the least bit cheerful; but they had no notion how gloomy they were shortly going to be. For it was not until they were right inside No. 27, with the door shut, that Nana gave a more downright danger-bark than ever, and the voice of the tiniest star, that can't be seen except through a powerful telescope, cried out across the sky:

'Now, Peter!'

As the stars are not really friends with Peter (who is much too fond of trying to blow them out), this shows they were watching eagerly that night, under the impression that something extra interesting was about to happen.

They were quite right. It did happen.

Chapter Three

A Strange Disappearance

The three little Darlings were peacefully asleep. They heard neither Nana nor the star: they never saw their three nightlights blink and go out, one after another. Still less did they see the extraordinary light that was darting and dashing about the room, hunting in every drawer and cupboard, hole and corner – searching for Peter's shadow.

This light, which was like a ball of fire when it moved, was a fairy when it stood still. It was a fairy-girl, about as long as one's hand, dressed in a delicate skeleton-leaf. Whenever she spoke she made a lovely tinkling noise like little golden bells: for this reason she was called Tinker Bell. After she had flashed all round the place, she disappeared into a jug. The next moment, Peter Pan dropped in through the open window. He knew his way about very well, you see. But Tinker Bell (whom he had had to carry) had never been in a nursery before. She found it extremely interesting: especially the jug. 'Tink, where are you?' Peter whispered softly, 'Tink, have you found where they have put my shadow?'

She answered him in the tinkling fairy language, 'Yes, it's on the big box,' by which she meant the chest of drawers. They both rushed at the chest. Peter pulled out his shadow, and unrolled it in such haste that he never noticed he had left Tinker Bell shut up in the drawer where it had been.

He thought his shadow would hurry to join itself on to him again: but it didn't. It did not, indeed, seem to recognise him at all, and kept aloof. Perhaps, being rolled up had affected it in some way. He got some soap from the bathroom, and tried to stick it on with that, but it slithered off again. Peter sat down and sobbed. Fancy recovering one's shadow, only to find that it could do without you!

The sound of his weeping wakened Wendy. She sat up and

enquired politely, 'Why are you crying, little boy?'

Peter, who had lovely manners when he liked, jumped up and made a beautiful bow to Wendy. She returned it, as well as she could in bed. He asked her, 'What's your name?'

'Wendy Moira Angela Darling,' she replied, feeling that this sounded very nice. 'What's your name?'

'Peter Pan.' It sounded too short after hers: both of them noticed that.

Wendy wanted to know where he lived: and he told her, 'Second turn to the right, and then straight on till morning.'

'What a funny address!' said Wendy. 'I mean, is that what they put on your letters? – or your mother's letters?'

Peter explained that he had no letters, and no mother, and no shadow – at least, the shadow wouldn't stick on. When Wendy discovered that he had been trying to fix it with soap, she was inclined to laugh. 'It must be *sewn* on, of course,' she said: and she got out of bed, fetched her work-basket, and sewed the shadow on to his feet.

This hurt a bit, of course: but Peter was soon jumping about in wild delight, crowing with conceitedness, and boasting, 'Oh! the

cleverness of me!' – as if he had put the shadow on by himself.

'Well,' exclaimed Wendy, shocked, 'of all the cocky, conceited boys! Of course *I* did nothing!'

'Oh, you did a little, perhaps,' he answered carelessly.

'A little!' repeated Wendy, and she returned to her bed in a dignified manner, covering up her head with the blankets. Peter was rather alarmed. He told her he couldn't help crowing when he was pleased with himself, and that one girl was more use than twenty boys.

This melted Wendy's heart. She came out of the blankets again, and sat with Peter on the side of the bed. She also offered to give him a kiss if he liked: and Peter held out his hand for it. Wendy saw at once that the poor boy had never had a kiss: so, not to hurt his feelings, she took off her thimble and put it on his finger. He was ever so pleased. 'Now, shall I give you a kiss?' he asked: and he dropped into her hand an acorn button off his coat. Wendy fastened it on to the little chain she wore round her neck. It was a hard sort of kiss: but so was her thimble.

'How old are you, Peter?' she said. This was a most uncomfortable question for him.

'I don't know,' he stammered, 'but quite young, anyhow . . . You see, Wendy, I ran away the day I was born, because I heard my father and mother talking about what I was to be when I grew up.'

'Dear, dear!' said Wendy – he must have been a very brave baby, she thought.

'I don't want to grow up ever!' he continued excitedly. 'I don't want to be a man. I want to stay a little boy, and have fun. That's why I ran away and lived with the fairies in Kensington Gardens.'

Wendy was intensely interested. Imagine talking to a boy who knew fairies! She asked so many questions about fairies that Peter was astonished, for he found them rather commonplace; and indeed sometimes they were such a nuisance, he had to scold them. He did his best, however, to give her all possible information. 'You see, Wendy,' he said, 'when the first baby laughed for the first time, its laugh broke into a thousand pieces, and they all went skipping about, and that was the beginning of fairies. But there aren't many of them now: they're mostly dead. It's because children have left off believing in them, you know. Every time a child says, "I don't believe in fairies," another fairy somewhere falls down dead.'

Here Peter suddenly remembered Tinker Bell. Could she have

fallen down dead? She was certainly very quiet. 'I can't think where she has gone to. Tink! Tink!' – and he looked about him.

'You don't mean to say there's a fairy in this room!' cried Wendy, clutching his arm.

'Well, she was here just now,' said Peter. They both looked and listened. A tiny tinkle of bells came from the chest of drawers: and Peter burst into a gurgle of laughter. 'Oh Wendy!' he whispered, 'I do believe I shut up poor Tink in the drawer!'

He let Tink out, and she flew about the room, perfectly wild with fury. 'I'm sorry,' said Peter, 'but how could I know you were in the drawer?' Tink dashed to and fro in a fearful passion, and at last settled down a moment upon the cuckoo clock, so that Wendy saw her and cried out, 'O the lovely! What is she saying, Peter?'

'She's not in a good temper,' he explained. 'She says she is my fairy, and that you are a great ugly girl.'

'Oh!' said Wendy, distressed.

'But you're talking nonsense, Tink,' said Peter. 'You know you are. You can't be my fairy, because I am a gentleman and you are a lady.'

Tink replied, 'You silly ass,' and vanished into the bathroom.

Peter apologised for her bad behaviour. 'She is quite a common fairy,' he told Wendy, 'she doesn't know any better. She is called Tinker Bell, because she mends the pots and kettles.' This was something he had just invented. Fortunately Tink did not hear it.

'Then, Peter,' said Wendy, 'where do you live now? In Kensington Gardens?'

'Well, sometimes I do. But mostly I live with the Lost Boys.'

'Who are they?'

'Why, the children who fall out of their prams when the nurses are looking another way. If nobody claims them in seven days, they are sent to the Neverland. I'm captain of them.'

'What fun!' exclaimed Wendy. 'Then, Peter, why do you come here to our nursery window?' She hoped he would answer, 'To see you,' – but he said it was to listen to her mother's stories. It's the same reason that makes swallows build nests in the eaves of houses. They are eavesdroppers. None of the Lost Boys had mothers, Peter went on, and none of them knew any stories, except what Peter overheard and brought back. And he only brought scrappetty bits, just shreds and patches of fairy tales – picked up by eavesdropping.

But when Wendy remarked that she knew lots of stories – and she told him the end of *Cinderella*, just to show him – Peter was struck by a dazzlingly bright idea. He proposed that she should come back with him to the Neverland and tell her stories to the Lost Boys: and darn their clothes, and make pockets for them, and tuck them in at night – and, in short, mother the Lost Boys properly. Anybody who has ever had a mother like Mrs Darling will understand at once how this notion tempted Wendy. She saw that she could be a sort of Mrs Darling No. Two.

And Peter went further still – oh, but he was artful! He promised to teach her to fly – to show her real mermaids with tails; he also mentioned pirates. John and Michael were awake by this time, listening with all their ears. They insisted on having a flying lesson at once.

But, at this point, everybody had to hide behind the window curtains. For Liza entered, in a very bad temper, dragging Nana with her. She had been making Christmas puddings in the kitchen: but Nana kept up such a miserable barking, that Liza had brought her to the nursery, just to see for herself that everything was all right. 'There!' she said angrily, 'they're perfectly safe. Lights out, and every one of the little dears sound asleep. Listen to their gentle breathing.' Here Michael overdid his gentle breathing, and made it so loud that it was plainly a pretence. Nana knew that sort of breathing; she tried to pull herself away from Liza. But Liza sternly marched her downstairs again, tied her up, and returned to the Christmas puddings.

The unhappy dog was determined to rescue the children from the danger that she felt was somewhere near. She strained and strained at her chain until it broke: and in another minute she was bursting into the dining room of No. 27 – where she knew her master and mistress had gone – with her paws flung up and an expression of despair. Mr and Mrs Darling saw at once that there was something dreadful happening at home. They didn't wait to say goodbye to their friends. They rushed out and followed Nana to No. 14.

Meanwhile, Peter had taught the three children to fly, after a fashion. At first they were decidedly clumsy – they would never be so elegant as Peter, who had been flying all his life. But he blew some fairy dust on them – and soon they flew quite well enough for young beginners. Round and round the room they went: it was quicker and easier every time. Mr and Mrs Darling, staring up at the nursery window as they ran along the street with Nana, saw three little figures in nightclothes circling round the room in a blaze of light. No, there were four figures! Oh, dear, what did it mean?

Before the distracted parents could reach the nursery door, three things had happened. Peter had mentioned mermaids and pirates again: the stars had blown the window open: and the four little figures had soared out into the night.

Peter went first, Michael and Wendy followed. John was last, because he had stopped to put on his Sunday hat.

Mr and Mrs Darling and the dog Nana rushed into the deserted nursery – just one moment too late.

Chapter Four

A Flight of Nestlings

When Peter told Wendy the way to his address in the Neverland, 'second to the right, and straight on till morning,' he was just saying the first thing that came into his head. He was like that. To tell the truth, he was no good at all as a guide. The children had been flying for days and nights, as it seemed, and not arriving anywhere: ever so many second-to-the-rights, and goodness knows how many mornings. They were sometimes too cold, then too warm: they were generally hungry, and sleepy all the time. Flying isn't such fun as they had fancied, when it goes on too long.

The bother was, if they went to sleep for one second, down they fell. Peter could go to sleep floating on his back, because he was so light: but he was always having to dive down and rescue John or Michael before they touched the sea. For now they were flying over the sea: and it seemed to have no shore anywhere. Peter was showing-off all the time – swooping away after birds, and down till he could touch the sharks' tails; or up among the stars, making jokes to them: but the children were constantly bumping into clouds, and he didn't seem to care. Indeed, he did not always remember who they were, and was inclined to pass them by. It sounds heartless; but, as has been already remarked, Peter was like that. It was merely want of thought, not of heart. He had had no mother to train him. And when Michael, having unthinkingly shut his eyes, suddenly dropped every now and then, Peter was not a bit alarmed – on the contrary, he thought it very funny. Besides, it gave him another chance of showing-off.

However, though the journey was very long, there came at last an evening when Peter remarked quite calmly, 'There it is!' The children knew what he meant: the magic island, the Neverland. It had been looking out for them and expecting them all this while.

They cried, 'Where, where?' He told them: 'Where all the arrows are pointing.' The setting sun was sending out a stream of golden rays, like arrows pointing at the island. Yes, sure enough, there was their dear old friend the Neverland. They recognised it at once. Indeed, they could not have mistaken it.

They could see the lagoon – the flamingoes – the upside-down boat – the wigwam – Wendy's orphan wolf – a Redskin camp in the distance. Everything they had ever made-believe about was there – it had come perfectly true. No doubt the pirates whom Peter had mentioned, and the mermaids, were somewhere around as well. You can't think how joyful Wendy, John and Michael were, as they stood on tiptoe in the air and showed each other all the different delightful things!

Peter was a trifle annoyed at their already knowing so much about the Island: he would have liked it to be more of a surprise, so that he could act as showman.

But then, suddenly, the sun sank out of sight: the golden arrows vanished: and the Island became all dark and gloomy. The children had noticed this happening at home: the Neverland always became a rather frightening place, about bedtime. There were too many shadows about, and the wild beasts and other enemies grew stronger and fiercer. So that they were often rather glad when Nana lit the nightlights, and told them that the Neverland was only make-believe.

But this wasn't make-believe, it was real: and it was getting more gloomy and shadowy every second – there were no nightlights, there was no Nana. None of the Darlings was sure that it was enjoying itself. Peter, however, was enjoying himself finely. He was no longer careless and forgetful, but full of excitement, and wanting to fight. And it was now so difficult to move along through the air, just as if somebody or something was pushing them back. Off and on, Peter beat his way with his fist, as if against unseen enemies.

'They don't want us to land,' he said.

Wendy asked him in a whisper, 'Who are they?' But he made no answer. He wakened Tinker Bell, who had been asleep on his shoulder, and made her go on in front.

Then he began to listen intently, poised in the air with his hand to his ear: or he would stare down with eyes like gimlets. It was not quite comfortable for the children: because plainly there was danger somewhere close at hand.

Presently Peter asked John, in an off-hand style: 'Do you want an adventure now, right away? Or would you rather have your tea first?'

'Tea first,' said Wendy hastily: but John wanted to know: 'What kind of adventure?'

'There's a pirate asleep just below us, in the pampas grass,' said Peter carelessly. 'If you like, we'll go down and kill him.'

John replied, after a long pause, that he didn't see the pirate. 'Besides,' he added, 'suppose he wakes up?'

Peter was very angry. 'Did you really think I should kill him while he was asleep? I always wake them before I kill them. Tons I have slain like that.'

'How ripping!' said John doubtfully. 'Are there many pirates on the island just now?'

'Never known so many.'

'Who is their captain?'

Peter answered with a stern face. 'Their captain is James Hook.'

Then Michael started blubbing, and John felt choky and gulpy. For they had heard of Hook, the worst pirate of all – a most terrible man to meet. And they wished they had not been so venturesome as to take flight to the Neverland with Peter. At least he might have warned them beforehand about Hook.

'He's not so big as he was,' observed Peter, trying to reassure them, 'I cut off a bit of him myself.'

'What bit?'

'His right hand.'

'Then he can't fight?'

'Can't he though! He has had an iron hook put on instead of his right hand: and he claws with it.'

'Oo – er!' said everybody.

'There's one thing,' continued Peter, 'that every boy who serves under me has to promise. Say "Ay, ay, sir,"' he snapped at John.

'Ay, ay, sir,' said John, who was feeling pale across his waist.

'If we meet Hook in open fight, don't attack him. Leave him entirely to me.'

'I promise, sir,' returned John obediently.

They now discovered that the pirates had sighted them, owing to the light of Tinker Bell (who was circling round and round them as they flew), and had got out their gun, Long Tom. 'They may let fly at us any moment now,' remarked Peter in his don't-carest manner.

The children were anxious, to put it mildly, on hearing this. They begged Peter to send Tinker Bell away – but he refused. 'She is rather frightened,' he said – 'she thinks we have lost the way. You don't think I would send her away all by herself when she is frightened!'

Wendy suggested that Tink should put her light out.

'She can't,' replied Peter, 'no fairy can. It just goes out by itself when she falls asleep.'

'Then tell her to go to sleep!' cried John.

'But she can't sleep unless she's sleepy. No fairy can.'

What was to be done? Peter suddenly suggested that they might place Tink in John's black top-hat, as nobody had a pocket to put her in. Not a spark of her light could be seen in the hat, which was carried by Wendy; and they flew on in darkness and silence: the only sounds being a lapping noise and a rasping noise, which, Peter remarked, were the wild beasts drinking at the ford, and the Redskins sharpening their knives.

These sounds were rather alarming: but when they ceased, it was altogether too quiet: and Michael exclaimed:

'It's so lonely: I do wish something would make some noise!'

Crash! – That was the firing of Long Tom.

Bangggg! – That was the echo, roaring all round the mountains.

Oo! – That was three gasps rolled into one.

Nobody knew whether he or she had been hit: but, as a matter of fact, it was even worse than that. For Peter had been blown far out to sea by the wind of the shot: Wendy had been blown upwards, still clutching the hat with Tinker Bell in it: and John and Michael were alone in the darkness: not sure how much of them was left, or if they were partly in pieces.

Now, it would have been a good thing if Wendy had let the hat fall, Tinker Bell and all. For Tink, like other fairies, had so small a mind that it could only hold one feeling at a time. The feeling which was now filling it, was furious jealousy of Wendy. She flew out of the hat and darted to and fro, tinkling most exquisitely: and Wendy understood that lovely tinkle to mean, 'It's all right, only follow me!' It didn't, though. It meant, 'I hate you!'

Wendy called desperately to Peter, to John, to Michael. No answer. So of course she followed Tink.

Chapter Five

The Island and the Islanders

Whenever Peter was away from the Neverland, everybody there slacked off and took things easy. But when he was known to be returning, the island woke up and became full of energy. At the present moment the Lost Boys were busy looking for Peter, the Pirates were busy looking for the Lost Boys. The Redskins were busy looking for the Pirates, and the wild beasts were busy looking for the Redskins. They were moving round and round the island after each other: but as all were going at the same rate, in the same direction, they did not overtake each other and they did not meet. This was quite a change for everybody: for during Peter's absences, things were so slack that the Pirates and Boys, if they met, merely bit their thumbs at each other.

There were at this time six boys on the island: they were stealing along in single file, wrapped in the skins of bears which they had killed. Each had his hand on his dagger, and each looked a trifle bloodthirsty, though he was not particularly feeling so.

The first boy was Tootles, a kind, humble, melancholy creature, who never met with anything but ill luck. The next was the cheerful Nibs: then the lively Slightly, intensely conceited, but nothing like so conceited as his captain, Peter. The fourth boy, Curly, was always in scrapes and mischiefs; he was sure to be blamed if anything went wrong, and was pretty safe to deserve it. Then came the Twins: and as Peter did not know one from the other, it couldn't be expected that anybody else would. The Twins, indeed, were quite uncertain themselves as to which was which: but they always kept close together, lest they should become more bewildered still.

A little while after the boys had passed, came a sound of villainous singing. It was impossible to mistake it for any song but the

Pirates' bloodcurdling ditty:

> *'Avast, belay, yo ho, heave to,*
> *A-pirating we go,*
> *And if we're parted by a shot,*
> *We're sure to meet below.'*

A shocking set of scoundrels prowled stealthily on the track of the Lost Boys: Cecco the Italian, the Blackamoor Man, Bill Jukes, Cookson, Gentleman Starkey, Skylights, Robert Mullins, Alfred Mason, the Irish bo'sun Smee (not a bad sort), Noodles, whose hands were fixed on backwards, and many other ruffianly rascals: some tattooed, some ear-ringed, some scarred; each completely armed with pistols, cutlasses, muskets, daggers, and extremely hideous to behold.

Anybody would have run a mile to escape from this horrible crew. But they were treated like mere dogs by their captain, James Hook, who was the biggest and most dreadful of them all. He lay in a rough chariot which was pushed and pulled by his men: smoking two cigars at once by means of a clever contraption he had invented, and waving his terrific iron claw. The most unpleasant thing about Hook (next to the iron claw) was his politeness: the more dangerous he was, the politer he grew. And there was only one thing on earth of which he was afraid – that was, the sight of his own blood.

A few minutes after the Pirate horde had disappeared, there
followed the Redskins, of the Piccaninny tribe: their bodies painted and
oiled, their eyes gleaming. They were armed with knives and
tomahawks, and decorated with strings of scalps. Their chief brave,
Great Big Little Panther, went ahead on all-fours: the beautiful princess
Tiger Lily strode proudly in the rear. The Redskins moved in perfect

silence, the only noise being a rather heavy breathing. Otherwise they were soundless as shadows.

On their heels, very shortly, came a hungry procession of wild beasts, man-eaters of the fiercest kind, of lions, tigers, bears, and a variety of smaller savage animals, all with their tongues hanging out: a sight to make one shiver.

And last of all, leisurely, waddling and wriggling by itself, crawled a gigantic Crocodile.

Each of these parties was keeping a sharp look-out in front: but none of them ever thought that danger might be creeping up behind.

The six Lost Boys fell out of the march first. They threw themselves on the grass, close by their underground dwelling, and talked about Peter and the stories he brought back to tell them. All too soon, however, they heard an ominous chanting in the distance: they recognised the Pirate song, slowly but surely drawing nearer. And at once they disappeared, like so many rabbits: except Nibs, who went scouting.

For seven large trees were there, each with a large hole in its hollow trunk; and these were the doorways to the Lost Boys' home beneath the sward, which Hook, for all his searching, had never so far been able to find.

As the Pirates approached, however, the ferocious Starkey spied Nibs slipping among the trees – and he pulled out his pistol. But Hook clawed his shoulder, and ordered him to put back his weapon. 'Do you want to bring Tiger Lily's Redskins on us, and to lose your scalp?' demanded Hook in his black and threatening voice. 'That boy is only one. I want to capture all the seven. Scatter round, men, and search for them.'

When the obedient Pirates were scattered about the wood, Captain Hook was left alone with his bo'sun, Smee. He talked to him long and earnestly, telling the whole story of his evil adventurous life. But Smee could not make head or tail of it. The only part he understood was when Hook began to speak of Peter Pan.

'It was he who cut off my arm,' said Hook with dark looks. 'Oh, I'll tear him for that!' he brandished the iron claw. 'He flung my arm to a Crocodile that happened to be passing by.'

'I have often noticed your curious fear of crocodiles,' said Smee.

'Not of crocodiles in general,' replied Hook. 'Only of that one

Crocodile.' Then he continued in a hoarse whisper – 'Smee, listen – It liked my arm so much that it has been following me ever since by land and sea, licking its lips for the rest of me.'

'It's a sort of compliment, you might say,' said Smee.

'I don't want compliments!' snapped Hook. 'What I want is to get hold of Peter Pan!' He sat down, as he spoke, upon a large mushroom. 'That Crocodile would have had me long ago,' he went on, 'but luckily it once swallowed a clock. The clock keeps on ticking inside it, and so I hear the tick-tick, and escape before it can reach me. Ho, ho!' and he gave a hollow laugh.

'Sooner or later,' said Smee, 'the clock will run down, and then—'

'Ay, that's it,' groaned Hook. 'The clock must stop some day, and then—' He jumped up. 'This seat is hot! I'm all but burning! What ails the thing? A red-hot mushroom!'

They examined the mushroom carefully: they pulled at it, and it came away in their hands. There was no root there – only a hole, from which smoke ascended. The two Pirates stared at the smoke and at each other, and they exclaimed with one voice – 'A chimney!'

Sure enough, it was the chimney of the Lost Boys' house underground. They always kept it stopped up with a mushroom if enemies were lurking near. Their merry voices could be heard quite plainly down below: they thought they were perfectly safe there. The Pirates replaced the mushroom, and soon perceived the holes in the seven hollow trees. The boys had mentioned, in their innocent cheerful prattle, that Peter Pan was away: both Hook and Smee had heard them. And Hook stood a long while meditating: he was plainly thinking of some criminal plan. Smee was all impatience to know it. At length Hook spoke, slowly through his clenched teeth.

'We will return to the ship,' said he with a horrid smile, 'and cook a large rich cake with green sugar on top, very thick and tempting. We will leave this cake on the shore by the Mermaids' Lagoon. These boys will find the cake, for they are always swimming about there, and they will gobble it up. You see, they have no mother, and they don't know how dangerous it is to eat rich damp cake – Ha! ha! – and so they will all die!' Hook roared with laughter: so did Smee. 'The prettiest plot that ever I heard!' cried Smee. And they danced and sang together.

In the midst of their wicked exultation, however, their singing was checked by a very, very tiny, but very distinct sound – gradually coming nearer – nearer – clearer – clearer:

Tick tick tick tick.

'The Crocodile!' gasped Hook, shuddering violently. And he bounded away in desperate alarm. Smee followed him.

Yes, it was the Crocodile. It had got past the Redskins, who were tracking the other Pirates, and was trailing itself along after Hook.

There was now a moment's breathing-space, and the boys came up to the open air again – but they were scarcely above ground, when Nibs rushed in among them with a pack of howling wolves behind him.

'Save me!' cried Nibs; and he fell exhausted.

The boys had no weapons that would keep off wolves: but they were extremely brave: and they said to each other, through the baying of the wolves, 'What would Peter do?' Then they immediately answered themselves, 'He would look at them through his legs.'

The five boys (for Nibs still lay on the ground) stooped down and advanced backwards upon the wolves, glaring at them between their legs. The wolves, after one long moment of hesitation, turned tail and fled.

Nibs picked himself up. 'There's a great white bird,' he cried. 'It's flying this way, and it moans as it flies. A wonderful thing!'

'What kind of bird? What does it say?'

'I don't know,' said Nibs, 'I never saw one like it. It moans, "Poor Wendy!"'

'There are birds called Wendies,' observed Slightly.

'There it comes!' exclaimed the boys. 'Hullo, there's Tink!' They saw her light flashing to and fro. Wendy was almost overhead, they heard her plaintive cries – mingled with the shrill tinkle of the jealous Tinker Bell, who was darting at Wendy and pinching her savagely, all the time, at one side and another.

When she was near enough to the boys, she shrieked out to them, 'Peter wants you to shoot the Wendy. Quick, quick!'

The boys were accustomed to doing whatever Peter commanded. While they rushed to fetch their bows and arrows, Tootles, who had his weapons with him, cried, 'Tink, get out of the way!' and he aimed and shot, in great excitement.

Wendy came falling to the earth with an arrow in her breast.

Chapter Six

The Little House

'I have shot the Wendy!' cried Tootles to the other boys, as they appeared out of the hollow trees. 'Look, there it lies. Won't Peter be pleased with me!' Tootles considered himself quite a hero.

'Silly ass!' said Tinker Bell as she darted to hide herself. The boys crowded round the body of Wendy.

'But this isn't a bird!' said Slightly, with a scared expression.

'What is it, then?' said Tootles, alarmed.

'I believe it's a lady,' said Slightly. You must remember none of the Lost Boys had seen a lady, because they could not recollect their

own mothers. All they knew about ladies was through the stories which Peter brought home.

'If it is a lady, we have killed her,' said Nibs.

'Peter was bringing her to us, very likely,' said Curly.

'A lady to take care of us at last,' said one Twin.

'And now you have killed her,' said the other Twin.

They were sorry for Tootles, but much sorrier for themselves. It did not occur to them to be sorry for Wendy.

Tootles was white and trembling. He said, 'Yes, I did it. I have only seen ladies in dreams, and when one really came, I have shot her. Oh, what will Peter say?'

Then they heard a joyful crowing noise aloft, and they knew it was Peter returning. They tried to hide the body of Wendy, by gathering closely round it – all except Tootles.

Peter it was. He dropped lightly beside them, and cried, 'Greeting, boys!' They saluted in silence.

'Why don't you cheer?' he asked, frowning. 'I have great news for you, boys. I have brought a mother for all of you.'

There was no answer.

'Haven't you seen her?' enquired Peter uneasily. 'She was flying this way.' Then Tootles showed him Wendy lying there with the arrow in her breast.

Peter was thoroughly uncomfortable. He was also quite at a loss how to act: whether to treat it as a joke, or to take no notice, or what. But it would never do to let his band see that he was uncertain about the next step.

'She is dead,' he said at last. Nobody wished to contradict him. There seemed little else to say.

'Perhaps she is frightened at being dead,' he continued. The rest had no remarks to make. The whole matter was quite beyond them.

Peter drew the arrow out of Wendy, and demanded, 'Whose arrow?' Tootles, meekly kneeling, replied, 'Mine, Peter.' And, as Peter lifted the arrow to use it as a dagger, Tootles bared his breast to receive it.

Peter raised the arrow twice, but he appeared unable to stab Tootles with it. 'Something stays my hand,' he muttered.

They were all gazing hard at him, except Nibs: who luckily was looking at Wendy. Nibs saw her move her arm. He bent over her and exclaimed in an awestruck whisper, 'She spoke! She said, "Poor Tootles!"'

'She is alive,' said Peter.

'The Wendy lady is alive!' cried Slightly.

Peter knelt beside her, and found that the arrow had struck against the acorn button which he had given her in the nursery, and which she had put upon her neck-chain. He showed it to the boys. 'It is the kiss I gave her. It has saved her life.'

From overhead there came a dismal wailing: it was Tinker Bell crying because her cruel plan had failed. The boys had to tell Peter all about it. He was very stern indeed. 'Tink,' he said, 'I am no longer your friend. Begone from me for ever.'

She pleaded hard, but he brushed her off his shoulder. Then Wendy was seen to move her arm again: it may have meant 'Poor Tink!' – for she was a very forgiving girl. So Peter said, 'Well, not for ever, but for a whole week,' – and Tink went off. Peter, as has been mentioned, often had to scold the fairies, for being so annoying: and Tink deserved a scolding more than any.

The puzzle was, what to do with Wendy, who was still in a

fainting state. Slightly thought it would not be respectful to carry her down into the underground home: yet he agreed that if she were left lying where she was, she would most likely die. Peter had one of his brilliant ideas. He said, 'Let us build a little house around her!' And he sent the boys hurry-scurry in every direction, for building material, bedding, firewood, and the best things that they had got underground. In the midst of this bustle and commotion, there appeared two drowsy figures, who fell asleep between every two steps they walked – John and Michael.

'Hullo, Peter!' they hailed him. 'Is Wendy asleep?'

'Hullo,' said Peter, who had forgotten that there were any such people as John and Michael. 'Yes, she's asleep.'

Michael proposed that they should waken her to get some supper for them. But Peter ordered that these two new boys were to help in building the house.

'Ay, ay, sir.'

'Build a house,' said John. 'Where? Why? Who for?'

'For the Wendy,' replied Curly.

'For Wendy!' repeated John. 'Why, she is only a girl.'

'Away with them!' said Peter. So the astonished brothers were made to work, and carry furniture, and obey orders: no easy matter when one is more than three-quarters asleep.

Meanwhile Slightly pretended to be a doctor come to cure Wendy: he borrowed John's hat for this. When he appeared, looking very solemn, Peter asked him, 'Please, sir, are you a doctor?'

'Yes, my little man,' replied Slightly: who was not quite sure whether Peter would approve of this make-believe, or would rap him on the knuckles.

'Please, sir, there is a lady lying very ill,' said Peter.

'Where is the lady?' enquired Slightly, taking care not to notice Wendy at his feet. When she was pointed out to him, he said, 'I will put a glass thing in her mouth,' and made-believe to do so. Peter waited anxiously till the glass thing was taken out. 'How is she?' he asked.

'This has cured her,' answered Slightly. Peter said he was very glad.

'I will call again this evening,' said Slightly; 'you must give her beef-tea out of a cup with a spout to it.' And he went away to take back the top-hat to John: puffing and blowing with relief, because nobody ever knew how much it was safe to make-believe with Peter. Peter did not seem to know what was real and what wasn't.

But, sure enough, Wendy was getting better. The noises all around her, of chopping boughs and bringing furniture and building materials, had roused her. The boys saw her moving, and opening her mouth. Peter said, 'Perhaps she is going to sing in her sleep'; and he told her to sing the kind of house she would like to have.

Wendy sang, with her eyes still shut:

'I wish I had a pretty house,
The littlest ever seen,
With funny little red walls,
And roof of mossy green.'

In no time at all, they had built up the house over her: it was made of branches and moss, and nicely furnished with things from the underground house. The finishing touches were very clever: they were, a door-knocker made of Tootles' shoe-sole, and a chimney made of John's top-hat with the bottom out. When the boys saw smoke coming

out of the chimney, they knew it was a proper little house.

By Peter's orders, they all stood round outside the door, trying to look their best; while he knocked politely, and Tinker Bell sat sneering on a branch near by.

The door opened, and Wendy came out. They all pulled off their hats, and were delighted to see her surprise. 'Where am I?' she asked, wondering.

'We built this house for you,' said Slightly.

'This lovely, darling house!' exclaimed Wendy.

'And we are your children!' the Twins told her.

The boys went down on their knees (except, of course, John and Michael), and implored her, 'O Wendy lady, be our mother!'

Wendy was ever so pleased, but doubtful. She said, 'But, you see, I am only a little girl.'

'That doesn't matter,' said Peter airily. 'All we need is just a nice motherly person.'

'Well,' said Wendy, 'I am that, anyhow. I will do my best. Come indoors at once, children: I'm sure your feet are damp. And before I put you to bed, I will tell you the ending of *Cinderella*.'

Oh! what a jolly evening they had, all squeezed into the little house with the motherly Wendy! And how delicious it was to be tucked up in bed, in the home under the hollow trees! All night Peter kept guard (more or less) with a drawn sword outside Wendy's house, while the fairies (very inquisitive) peeked and pried around; while the Pirates caroused, and the wolves prowled in the distance. Nothing so happy and cosy as the little house looked, had ever been seen in the Neverland before.

Chapter Seven

Great Adventures

Peter, who was very wise by fits and starts, thought it would be safer for Wendy, John, and Michael to live, as a general rule, in the house below the ground: for he was under the delusion that this dwelling-place had never yet been discovered by Hook, and never would be. So he had the three newcomers measured for a hollow tree apiece, and after a little practice they were able to go up and down quite easily (it is done by a peculiar system of drawing-in and letting-out one's breath). And they simply loved the underground home. It was one large room, with strong mushrooms – excellent seats – springing out of the floor, and a sawn-off tree-trunk, which grew about two feet daily, and could be used as a table and then sawn down again. The fireplace was enormous, the bed was huge, and there was a tiny little recess in the wall, curtained off and exquisitely furnished, which was the apartment of Tinker Bell.

It was just as well that Wendy was so motherly, and so housekeeperly, and so fond of cooking, sewing, and mending; for, what with eight boys and Peter to look after, she had more than enough to do. Occasionally, for weeks together, she never put her nose above ground. She made them delicious meals of grated coconuts, baked pig, roasted bread-fruit, fried bananas, boiled yams and other splendid foods; but sometimes Peter chose to have a make-believe meal instead of a real one (it was all the same to him), and then the rest of the family had to go hungry till night, when Wendy would bring them secret platefuls in bed. After they were asleep, she always had any amount of patching and darning to do: as for the heeling of stockings, it was endless: but she enjoyed it. The pet orphan wolf, which she once had pretended about, had soon discovered her, and followed her continually. She was as happy as the day was long.

You may wonder, did Wendy never think of her dear father and mother, and Nana, and the nursery, left behind in England? Well, it was this way: she didn't worry. She felt sure they would leave the nursery window open, so that the children could return whenever they wished. It was unfortunate that John and Michael had such short memories. John could only remember his parents in a half-hearted way, and Michael was beginning to believe that Wendy was really his mother. She asked them questions, and set them examination papers about their old

home, in which the other boys joined without a hope of knowing the answers. But all the time, the three little Darlings went on forgetting more and more.

One reason was, that there were so many thrilling adventures: different ones every day. More than one can possibly tell: but all worth telling. For instance, there was the night attack by the Redskins, when several of them stuck in the hollow trees, and had to be pulled out like corks. There was Tinker Bell's attempt to kidnap Wendy, with the help of some low vulgar fairies – by having her, when asleep, conveyed to the mainland on a huge floating leaf. Luckily the leaf gave way, and Wendy awoke and swam back. There was the adventure of the Pirates' Cake, which they cooked, you will remember, so that the boys might perish after eating it. Wendy discovered this cake – cunningly concealed in one place after another – and rescued the children from its peril, so often, that in the end it left off being rich and juicy. It became as hard as a stone; and you could hit people with it: and Hook tripped-up over it in the dark. There was also the Lions' adventure, in which Peter, surrounded by roaring beasts, drew a magic circle round him on the ground with an arrow, and dared any lion to cross it. And there was the fight with the Redskins at the Gulch, when Peter suddenly changed sides, and made his band change too, so that, the Peterites having all become Redskins, the Redskins had, for the time being, to become Lost Boys.

These, and many more excitements – one a day at least – account for the mild nursery times fading out of people's memories. But the most remarkable adventure of all, perhaps, was the saving of Tiger Lily in the Mermaids' Lagoon. It happened like this:

The Mermaids lived in the lagoon, which was full of charming rainbow bubbles. They liked to bask upon Marooners' Rock, lazily combing out their long thick hair. They were not exactly shy, but they were not interested in Wendy and the boys. Peter would chat with them by the hour: yet if anybody else came along, the Mermaids would turn a cold shoulder, and splash a cold tail, and dive. They were decidedly unsociable to strangers.

One fine warm day, the children had all been swimming, and were now resting on Marooners' Rock after their dinner. Wendy was busy sewing: but, while she stitched, the sun went in, the air grew chilly, and so dark, she could not see to thread her needle. A shiver ran across

the water: certainly some danger was at hand. What was that soft chunk-chunk approaching? It was the sound of muffled oars.

Wendy would not waken the others, because she liked them to have a good half-hour's doze after their midday meal. But Peter always slept with one ear open. He gave a cry that roused the rest, as he sprang to his feet and listened.

'Pirates!' he cried: and 'Dive!' he shouted. The next instant, not a creature could be seen upon the Rock.

The Pirate dinghy, with its muffled oars, came up: there were three people in it, Smee the bo'sun, and the scoundrelly Starkey, and the beautiful Redskin Princess, Tiger Lily. Her wrists were tied together, so were her ankles. She knew she was going to be left to drown upon the Rock (which was submerged at high tide): but she was too proud to plead for mercy. She had been taken prisoner just as she was boarding the Pirate vessel with a knife in her mouth. Hook was going to make an example of her.

Peter and Wendy, keeping well out of sight, were bobbing up and down behind the Rock: Wendy was crying at the sad fate in store for

Tiger Lily. But Peter meant to save her: he knew he was clever enough to do it. And he imitated the voice of Hook. 'Ahoy there, you lubbers!' he bawled out of the dark.

'The captain!' cried the Pirates, but they could not perceive him anywhere. They supposed he must be swimming out to them. They answered him, 'We are just putting the Redskin on the Rock.'

They were greatly surprised at Hook's voice making reply, 'Set her free. Cut the cords. Let her go.'

'Free!' they gasped. 'But, captain, you ordered us—'

'Let her go at once!' bellowed the false Hook, 'or you shall feel my claw, I promise you!'

Smee and Starkey were utterly dumbfounded. They cut Tiger Lily's bonds, and she slipped like an eel into the water. Peter and Wendy were overjoyed for a moment: but in the same moment, the real Hook's voice rang over the lagoon, 'Boat ahoy! Boat ahoy!' The real Hook was swimming to the boat, and before the eyes of Peter and Wendy he reached it. He climbed in, and sat with his head on his hook, very gloomy and lost in thought.

The two Pirates asked, 'Is all well, captain?' But a hollow groan was the only answer. At last Hook answered violently, 'The game's up. We are beaten – beaten, I tell you! Those boys have found a mother!'

'What's a mother?' said Smee.

'He doesn't know!' exclaimed Wendy, thoroughly shocked. Peter pulled her down under the water, but Hook had already started up. 'What was that?' he cried.

Starkey lifted his lantern to light up the lagoon, but all they could see was the Never-Bird, sitting on her eggs in her floating nest, where she had been left undisturbed by Peter's command. The Pirates thought deeply. 'Captain,' said Smee, 'what if we should kidnap the boys' mother, and make her our own mother?'

'Glorious!' cried Hook. 'We will seize the boys and drown them, and take Wendy to be our mother.'

'Never!' cried Wendy from the water.

'What was that?' But Wendy had bobbed down again. The three Pirates climbed upon the Rock, and suddenly Hook demanded, 'Where is the Redskin girl?'

They supposed this was a little joke, and Smee answered with a chuckle, 'Oh, that's all right captain: we let her go, according to your orders.'

'You let her go!' yelled Hook.

'Why, you called across the water to us,' said Starkey. '"Cut her cords," says you, "and let her go."'

Hook went black in the face with fury: he was startled, too. There was something cheating and creepy about all this. 'I gave no such order,' said he.

'Most likely it was a spirit,' said Smee, shakily.

Hook raised his voice, and cried, 'What spirit haunts this dark lagoon? Spirit, hear me!'

Peter instantly replied, in the very voice of Hook himself, 'Odds bobs, hammer and tongs, I hear you.'

'Who are you?' demanded Hook.

The voice replied, 'I am James Hook, captain of the *Jolly Roger*.'

Hook shouted back, 'That you are not – you are not!'

The voice responded fiercely, 'Say that again, and I'll cast anchor in you.'

'If you are Hook,' exclaimed the Pirate captain, 'pray tell me, who am I?'

'A codfish – nothing but a codfish,' said the voice.

Smee and Starkey, who had been clinging together, drew back and regarded their leader with contempt. They muttered, 'Have we been captained by a codfish?'

Hook felt that he was losing hold of himself and of his men. He made a desperate attempt to recover. And suddenly a thought occurred to him. He cried out, 'Hook, have you another voice?'

Peter was taken off his guard. He answered gaily, in his own voice, 'I have.'

'And another name?'

'Yes.'

'Are you vegetable?' inquired Hook.

'No.'

'Mineral?'

'No.'

'Animal?'

'Yes.'

'Man?'

'No' (scornfully).

'Boy?'

'Yes.'

'Ordinary boy?'

'No.'

'Wonderful boy?'

'Yes.' For Peter was now at the very top of his conceitedness.

'Are you in England?'

'No.'

'Are you here?'

'Yes.'

'You'd better ask him some other questions,' said Hook to his comrades, 'I confess I am completely puzzled. This is no common spirit.'

'Can't think of anything to ask,' said Smee.

Peter began to crow. 'Can't guess, eh? Do you give it up?'

'Yes, yes!' they shouted.

'Well, then, I am Peter Pan!'

Oh, the disgust of Hook to find he had been beguiled by Peter! Oh, the joy of Hook to be once more in full command of his men and himself!

'We've got him now!' he roared. 'Take him, dead or alive!'

As Hook spoke, the voice of Peter cried, 'Are you ready, boys?' and 'Ay, ay, sir,' resounded from parts of the lagoon.

'Then lam into the Pirates! Give them what for!'

'Hurrah!' came the answer: and the short sharp fight began.

John tackled Starkey in the boat – presently both leapt overboard. Smee wounded Tootles, but was himself pinked by Curly. Starkey, having escaped from John, attacked Slightly and the Twins.

Meanwhile Peter was seeking his deadly enemy Hook. The Pirate captain, keeping everyone at bay with his iron claw, crawled out of the water to breathe, and climbed the slippery Rock. Here he came plump against Peter, who had scaled it from the other side. Peter was bursting with joy. He snatched a knife from Hook's belt, and was about to strike the villain, when he perceived that he was higher up the Rock than Hook was. It would not have been fighting fair to knife him. So he gave the Pirate a hand to hoist him up.

And Hook bit him.

The unfairness of this bite, just when he was acting nobly, took Peter completely by surprise. He could only stare, quite helpless with horror and amazement. Then the iron hand clawed him twice: and for a while he knew no more.

The third clawing would no doubt have done for the unconscious Peter, but rescue came from an unexpected quarter.

Tick tick tick tick.

Hook heard the dreadful sound – he knew that the Crocodile was close upon him. He leapt into the water, and struck out wildly for the ship, with the Crocodile in slow but sure pursuit.

By this time the boys, who had driven off Smee and Starkey, had found the dinghy and were going home in it, shouting 'Peter!' – and 'Wendy!' as they went. There was no answer, and they were a little uneasy, but not really anxious. They were sure neither Peter nor Wendy could come to any harm. Their calling died away in the distance. It was followed by a feeble cry, 'Help, help!'

Two little figures lay upon the Rock. Peter had drawn up Wendy there: she was in a faint. He fell beside her, fainting too. He saw that the water was rising and that they would soon be drowned, but it could not be helped: he was quite done for.

Presently a Mermaid caught hold of Wendy's feet, and was

pulling her gently into the water, when Peter roused up just in time to draw her back.

'The water will soon be over the Rock now, Wendy,' he told her, 'the Rock is getting smaller all the time.'

'We must go, then,' said Wendy. 'Shall we swim or fly back?'

'Could you swim or fly as far as the shore, Wendy, without me to help you?'

'No, I'm too tired.'

'But I can't help you, Wendy,' he moaned, 'I can neither fly nor swim. Hook has wounded me.'

'Oh, Peter! are you hurt? Then, you mean, we shall both be drowned?'

'Well, look how the water is mounting.'

They sat with their hands over their eyes, that they might not see the water coming up over them. And something brushed lightly against Peter – he caught hold of it, and it was the tail of Michael's kite. It had pulled itself out of Michael's hand some days before, and floated off. Now it had got some reason for returning. Peter saw the reason at once. He drew the kite in to him, and cried, 'It lifted Michael right off the

ground. I believe it could carry you back!'

'Both of us, Peter,' she answered.

'No, it can't lift two.' He had tied the tail round her while she was speaking.

Wendy clung to him, and refused to go without him. She wanted to cast lots as to who should stay on the Rock. But Peter was determined. He shoved her off: the kite took flight. She was lost to sight in a few minutes. Peter was left absolutely alone.

There was only a small space now for his feet to stand on. The moon rose pale above the waters: the Mermaids crooned wild songs to it. Everything was extraordinarily desolate. Peter had never been really-truly afraid in his life, but just for one shivery, trembly moment he was afraid now.

Then his fear passed, and he stood upright and smiling. Something was beating fast inside him; it might have been his heart, or it might have been a battle-drum. He would not have been surprised if there had been a bugle as well. It was going throb, throb, throb, and saying, 'To die will be an awfully big adventure.'

Chapter Eight

Ups and Downs

The waters rose steadily till they were touching Peter's toes: it would not be long before they swept him away. He watched, without interest, something that was moving on the lagoon: it looked like a piece of floating paper, very likely a bit of the kite. The queer thing was that it was going against the tide, and seemed to be trying to steer its course towards Peter.

When it came closer, he recognised that it was not a piece of paper, but the Never-Bird on her floating nest. She had come to try and save him: and she told him so. But Peter did not understand the bird-language, neither was she very good at his. So, the Never-Bird being exhausted with her efforts to reach him, and Peter being weak because of his wound, they bawled feebly at each other until each lost its temper at the other one's stupidity.

But the Never-Bird was a decent creature: and as Peter had been kind to her before, she was resolved to be grateful at all costs. She made one last effort, and pushed the nest against the Rock. Then she flew up off her eggs: and Peter understood at last. He waved his thanks as she hovered over him. She was watching to see what would happen to her two large white eggs. Peter was himself doubtful what to do with them.

But, as you know, he was never long at a loss for ideas. He perceived Starkey's hat, a deep, broad-brimmed, water-tight tarpaulin, hanging on a stave which jutted out of the Rock (having once marked the site of buccaneers' buried treasure). And he gingerly removed the eggs into this hat, and sent it afloat. It went beautifully. He then drew out the stave, set it in the nest for a mast, and put his shirt on it for a sail. The Never-Bird alighted on the hat, and sat comfortably on her eggs. She and Peter, both cheering, drifted in opposite directions.

Strange to say, Peter reached the house under the ground only a minute or two later than Wendy, who had been wafted to and fro by the kite. And they all sat up half the night, relating their enormous adventures.

After this eventful day, the Redskins became their particular friends. The rescue of Tiger Lily could not be repaid by mere thanks. So the Redskins stood on guard all night among the hollow trees: and by day they smoked the pipe of peace: and they bowed themselves to the earth before Peter, calling him the Great White Father. This pleased him immensely, and he addressed them in a lordly way as they grovelled at his feet. They took no notice of anyone else's feet, though: and they were inclined to speak of Wendy as a squaw: she did not approve of that.

One Saturday evening, the whole family was happily gathered together in the underground home, after a high tea (unfortunately a make-believe one). Wendy was busy with a great basket of stockings to mend, by no means make-believe. Peter had come in with his hands full of nuts for the boys: he had also been waiting near the Crocodile until its clock struck, so as to get the correct time for Wendy; she liked things

just so. He joined the children, who had put on their nighties, in a splendid dance-pillow-fight. They pretended to be scared of their own shadows, and whacked the shadows gloriously with pillows. Then Wendy, having put her family to bed, started telling them the story they loved best, and which Peter hated most. As a rule he left the room when she began it, or stopped his ears: but this time he stayed on his mushroom-stool; and listened – much against his will.

This story, which had no name, was about Mr and Mrs Darling, and their three children, and their faithful nurse called Nana. And it told how the children flew away one night, leaving their little empty beds; and how they stayed away for years, having a lovely time, because they knew the nursery window would always be left open for them to fly in again. And, in the very far end, they did return.

But Peter gave a hollow groan: so that Wendy ran to him anxiously, and asked: 'Where is it, Peter?' For it sounded like an indigestion, and a very sharp one at that.

Peter replied, 'It isn't the sort of pain you think. It is because I must tell you something that hurts. Wendy, you are quite wrong about mothers. I used to think the same as you do, that the window would always be left open. So I stayed away for ever so long. But when I flew back, my mother had forgotten me. The window was shut and fastened: and there was another little boy asleep in my bed.'

Wendy, John, and Michael heard this with horror. They cried to each other, 'Let us go home – tonight – at once!' They meant – 'before there's time to put other children in our beds.' The Lost Boys were terribly upset, and indeed were inclined to chain up Wendy, so that she would not forsake them. But Peter was more don't-carish than ever. He did not ask Wendy to stay, or show any feeling of any sort. She asked him to arrange for their going back, right away; and he took this request quite coolly and calmly. He went out forthwith, and instructed the Redskins to guide Wendy and her brothers through the wood: and he sharply ordered Tinker Bell to take them home across the sea.

As may be guessed, this was all swank and show-off on Peter's part. He minded Wendy's going so much that every inch of him felt tooth-achey. But he was not going to let her know it.

The motherly Wendy was very sore at Peter's never-minding, and at leaving the Lost Boys. She saw them looking so forlorn, that she invited them all to come home with her. 'I am almost sure,' she said, 'I can get my father and mother to adopt you.' Peter consented carelessly to this: but it turned out that *he* didn't intend to come. He wanted to remain a boy: and if he left the Neverland he might be obliged to grow up. Why grow up?

Wendy lingered by Peter, hoping he might yet be softened. She gave him particular instructions about his flannels and his medicine:

she expected a thimble (in other words a kiss), but Peter said goodbye as if she were a stranger who had just paid an hour's visit. None of

them had any more to say. It was wretched.

Tinker Bell rushed out to lead the way: and at that exact moment the Pirates, who had been stealthily massing in the wood, made their ferocious attack upon the unsuspecting Redskins.

Never was there a more deafening hullabaloo – shrieks, yells, war-whoops, curses, shots and clashes of steel trampling to and fro in furious combat!

In the house underground there was utter silence. Every face was turned towards Peter: every heart (except his) went bumpetty-bump. Peter seized his sword.

Sad to tell, the Redskins had been taken completely by surprise. By all the rules of honourable warfare, it was their business to attack the whites first, and that at dawn. They little dreamed that the unprincipled Hook would ambush them about 7 p.m. The consequence was, that they nearly all perished. Their Chief, Great Big Little Panther, with Tiger Lily and a mere handful of braves, cut a way through the victorious Pirates, and escaped into the farther woods.

Hook might well have shouted in triumph: but he stood apart in his usual mysterious gloom. It was not the Redskins whom he desired to destroy: it was Peter Pan. He listened above the chimney – and he heard Peter telling the others, 'If the Redskins have won, they will beat the tom-tom. That is their sign of victory.'

The Redskins had left their tom-tom behind: probably they knew that they would not require it. The treacherous Hook signed to Smee, the bo'sun, to beat it: and immediately the children began cheering down below, 'An Indian victory! Hurrah! Goodbye, Peter! Goodbye!' They came eagerly up their hollow trees – and fell straight into the clutches of the Pirates.

The boys were flung from hand to hand until they dropped at the feet of the Blackamoor Pirate, who trussed them and gagged them, one by one. There was no time for any to cry a warning to the others: so that Wendy, who came last, was thunderstruck at the sight she saw. Hook lifted his hat to her, offered her his arm, and led her, with horrid politeness, to witness the tying and gagging. The boys were thrown into the little house, and four Pirates bore it away to the shore, singing their hateful chorus as they went. The rest followed, chuckling in triumph.

Hook remained alone, plotting and planning. He had captured

eight boys and Wendy: but where was Peter Pan? After long thought, the Pirate captain let himself down the largest hollow tree. He found himself looking into the big underground room, with the great bed and the cheery fire. And on the bed lay Peter, sound asleep.

Peter had played on his pipes awhile, after the others left, to show himself that he did not care. He had not taken his *medicine* which Wendy had left all ready for him, because he thought it would annoy her if she knew. Then he had fallen asleep, not sure whether he was laughing or crying.

Hook could not get right into the room to make an end of Peter, as he wished: for a door, which he was unable to open, was at the bottom of the hollow tree. But he had a deadly poison, which he always carried about with him: and by making a long arm over the door, he was able to add five drops of this poison to Peter's glass of medicine. 'That's done for him!' he hissed. He crawled up the tree again, muffled himself in his cloak, and stole away again through the wood, muttering strangely.

Peter slept on for hours. He was wakened by a tapping at the door of

his tree: a soft and stealthy tapping. He cried, 'Who are you?' again and again, but no answer came: only the tapping was repeated. At last he heard a charming tinkle say, 'Let me in, Peter.'

Tink – for of course it was she – appeared, wildly excited. She told him, all in one breath, how Wendy and the boys were prisoners, bound and gagged upon the Pirate ship.

Peter sprang for his weapons: and he caught sight of his medicine. At least he could do one thing to please poor Wendy. He might not succeed in rescuing her: but at any rate he could take his medicine.

'No! don't touch it!' Tink shrieked. 'It's poisoned! Hook poisoned it!'

'Poisoned? Don't be so silly! How ever could he have got down here?'

'I heard him talking to himself in the forest,' said Tink. 'He was jolly well pleased with himself, too, because he had poisoned you.'

'Nonsense!' exclaimed Peter. 'Besides, I haven't been asleep.' He was just putting the cup to his lips, when Tink got there first, and swallowed it to the dregs. She looked very ill at once.

'O Tink, did you drink it to save me? Oh, why?'

'You silly ass!' she whispered: then she staggered to her little apartment, for her wings were failing, and lay limply on her bed. Her light grew fainter and dimmer: Peter, kneeling by her in sad trouble, knew that she was fading out. He cried like anything.

Then he just managed to make out what she was saying, in a tiny low voice, with the tinkle gone out of it – 'I think I could get well again if children believed in fairies.'

Peter raised his hands and cried out to all the children in the world (especially those who might be dreaming of the Neverland): 'Do you believe in fairies? Clap your hands if you do! Don't let Tink die! Quick! Say you believe in fairies!'

Then there was a distant clapping: it sounded from everywhere all around. Tink heard it, and it cured her instantly. She recovered her voice, she recovered her light – she jumped out of bed. She was as cheery and as cheeky as ever. How topping, to get well so quickly! That's what comes of being a fairy. It also comes of being believed-in. When Peter, fully armed, arose from his tree, the ground was white with snow. The Crocodile went trickling past him. Otherwise there was no sign of any living thing.

'This time,' said Peter, who was frightfully happy, 'it is Hook's life or mine!' And he set out, in the highest possible spirits, to rescue the boys and Wendy.

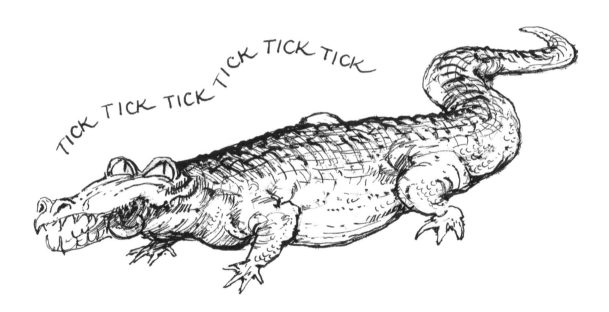

Chapter Nine

The Crocodile Wins

ear the mouth of the Pirate river lay an old, ill-looking vessel with raking masts. It was Hook's brig, the *Jolly Roger*: one could tell that at first sight. She showed a green riding-light: for the rest, she was dark and silent. The only sound audible aboard her was the whirr of the ship's sewing-machine, which was being worked by the bo'sun, Smee. The other Pirates were sprawling about in clumsy attitudes: some were fagged-out by carrying the little house with all the children in it, and some were gambling heavily – it was their only amusement.

Hook slowly paced the deck, dark and moody as usual. He had

(as he flattered himself) poisoned Peter: he was about to destroy all the other boys. And yet he felt no gladness: he hated everybody, including himself. Presently, noticing that his crew were inclined to be more cheerful, and that some of them had even started a song and dance, he became deeply enraged, and ordered the prisoners to be dragged up from the hold.

The eight boys, all chained so that they could not fly away, were ranged before the Pirate captain. He gave them a scornful glance, and said, 'Six of you have got to walk the plank tonight' – (at the end of the plank was the bottomless ocean) – 'but I can do with a couple of cabin boys. Which of you has the gumption to join the *Jolly Roger*?'

Wendy (who was still down in the hold) had told her family not to anger Hook more than they could help. So the Lost Boys were very polite in explaining, one after another, 'Well, sir, I don't think my mother would like me to be a Pirate.' Mothers come in very handy at awkward times like this.

Hook turned to John and Michael. He asked, had neither of them ever *wanted* to be Pirates? John was too truthful to deny it. He said that he had once thought of calling himself Red-handed Jack: and

Hook was satisfied at this reply. 'That shall be your name,' he assured John.

'What name should I have?' enquired Michael. Hook answered immediately, 'Blackbeard Joe.'

'What do you think?' the two boys questioned each other.

'I suppose we shall still be subjects of the King?' said John.

'Oh, no,' said Hook, savagely, 'you would have to say, "Down with the King!" before you became cabin boys, and at every opportunity afterwards.'

'Then I refuse,' cried John.

'Same here,' said Michael.

'Rule Britannia!' exclaimed Curly.

Hook bellowed at them, 'Your doom is sealed! Get the plank ready. Fetch up their mother to see their fate.' The men flew to obey him.

Wendy was distressed, of course, and afraid, of course: but still more she was disgusted. The dinginess of the ship, the dirtiness of the decks, the dishes, the Pirates' clothes, and everything else, made her full of contempt for such a slovenly lot of lazybones. She looked disdainfully at Hook.

'You are to see your children walk the plank,' he snarled. 'Let us hear a mother's last words to her children!'

'My dear boys,' said Wendy, 'here is a message from your real mothers. They say, "We hope our sons will die like English gentlemen."'

'We shall!' they cried, feeling much better for these brave words. 'We shall do what our mothers hope.'

'Tie her up to the mast!' yelled Hook.

'I'll save you yet,' whispered Smee as he tied her, 'if you'll promise to be *my* mother.'

'I would rather have no children at all,' said Wendy coldly.

The boys stared and shivered as they saw the plank which they must walk, one by one: and Hook, with a fiendish grin, moved towards Wendy. He meant to keep her face turned towards it, that she should not lose an inch of the dreadful sight. But just as he was about to claw her head round that way—

Tick tick tick tick.

Hook wilted and fell in a crumpled heap. And everyone was thinking the same ghastly thought: 'The Crocodile is climbing aboard

the ship!' There was no escape.

Hook, on his hands and knees, crawled as far as he could go, crying 'Hide me!' – and his crew gathered closely round him. They had no heart to fight. If the Crocodile was coming, it must come. They could not cope with it.

The boys rushed to the side to see the Crocodile climbing, and behold, there was not the ghost of a crocodile. It was Peter, ticking like mad. He signed to them to keep quite silent, and went on ticking and mounting. He had, indeed, been ticking so long that night, that he hardly knew he was doing it. At first he had done it to keep the wild beasts from attacking him; but later on it became mere force of habit. A Pirate came up from the fo'c'sle – and Peter was on him before he could squeak. His body was instantly cast overboard. The other Pirates began to look around, hearing the splash it made. Had the Crocodile changed its mind and jumped down again?

Peter disappeared into the cabin. There was not a tick in hearing. 'It's gone,' said Smee.

Hook stood up: and, to punish the children for their having seen him such a cowardy custard, he ordered that they should be flogged with the cat-o'-nine-tails before they walked the plank. They begged for pity, on their knees: but this only amused the loathsome Pirates.

'The cat's in my cabin,' said Hook. 'Fetch it, Jukes.'

'Ay, ay, sir.' These werc the last words Jukes ever uttered. For, while Hook and his crew were chanting their Pirate song for sheer malignant joy, a frightful screech arose from the cabin: followed by a high, weird crowing sound.

Cecco, the Italian, pushed into the cabin, and staggered out, white and trembling.

'Bill Jukes is in there, stabbed,' he gibbered, 'and that crowing thing is there, too. Something very wrong, says I.'

Hook perceived the alarm of his men and the delight of the boys. He was infuriated. 'Go back,' said he to Cecco, 'and bring me out that doodle-doo.' Cecco was for refusing, but Hook threatened him with the iron claw. In another minute (for Cecco did not hurry) there was another awful screech – another triumphant crow.

Hook now ordered Starkey to fetch him the doodle-doo: but that blackhearted ruffian defied his captain. And, when Hook's claw was already at his throat, he actually leapt into the sea rather than dare the Thing in the cabin.

So Hook went in himself, with a lantern: it was instantly blown out. He tottered back to his gang, and they all but jeered him. They marked his green and pallid looks.

The children, however, did not jeer – they cheered. And Hook was resolved to revenge himself on them. He had them driven into the cabin, and the door shut on them. 'Let them fight the doodle-doo for their lives,' cried Hook. 'If they all get killed, what matter? It will save us trouble in the long run.'

Peter had discovered in the cabin the key which would unlock the children's chains. He freed every one of them, and armed them with any weapons he could find. They stole out: and Peter cut the cords that bound Wendy to the mast. He bade them all hide, while he stood in Wendy's place by the mast, wrapped closely in her cloak. There he sent forth a mighty, magnificent crow.

The Pirates took this to mean that the Terror in the cabin had killed the whole eight of the boys. They were quaking and quailing with fright. They declared that the ship was doomed, that they were all done for: that there was a Jonah aboard, and that they thought he was a man with a hook.

'No, no,' exclaimed Hook, 'it's that girl there. Always brings a Pirate ship bad luck, it does, a woman aboard. Fling her to the fishes!'

They rushed at the cloaked figure by the mast. 'Nobody can save you now!' they mocked.

'One can,' was the answer.

'And who may that be?'

'Peter Pan!' and he threw off the cloak.

Then the Pirates began to understand the wild happenings in the cabin. Hook was at first too flabbergasted for speech. At last he called upon his men to 'Cut him to pieces!' – but that was easier said than done. Peter summoned his hidden boys, and a desperate fight took place. The Pirates were already depressed and disheartened. They ran to and fro, with no distinct idea who was attacking them – they fell easy victims to the boys and Peter. At length all were accounted for but one.

That one, needless to say, was Hook. He stood at bay among a ring of enemies, having grabbed one boy, whom he was using as a shield – when a light figure sprang face to face with him, and cried to the rest,

'Put up your swords. This man is mine!'

Peter was smiling strangely: Hook was shivering slightly. For some time they stared into each other's eyes. Hook was a heavy, hefty, large-built man. In size, in age, in cunning, he was six times a match for Peter. It was impossible that this boy could defeat him. Yet he had a shrewd suspicion that he would be overcome at last.

'So this is all your doing, is it?' said he, waving a claw towards his bloodstained decks.

'Ay, James Hook, it is all my doing,' answered Peter, crowing in his heart, though not aloud.

'You will live to regret it,' remarked Hook, as he threw himself madly upon his foe. The last battle had begun.

He had never supposed that Peter was so superb a swordsman. Neither his hook nor his blade gained any advantage for him: and presently Peter got under his guard and pierced him in the ribs. When Hook saw his own blood flowing, he was no longer his own man: it was, you may remember, the one thing that dismayed him. His sword slipped from his hand.

The boys screamed out – 'Now! At him, Peter! Finish him.' But Peter signed to Hook to pick up the sword.

The second bout was even fiercer than the first. Peter wounded Hook again and again. The Pirate captain was fighting without hope.

Suddenly he cried, 'Pax a moment,' and, rushing to the powder-magazine, he fired it. Then, with a snort of triumph, he told the crowding boys, 'In two minutes we shall all be blown to bits.'

But Peter had followed him to the powder-magazine: he now came out with the lighted fuse in his hands, and flung it overboard.

Then, as he advanced upon Hook, flying above him, his dagger poised to strike, the captain sprang upon the bulwarks, and with a sneer at Peter, plunged into the sea. The Crocodile was waiting for him just below: but this he did not know until he got there.

Chapter Ten

Many Happy Returns

It took a good night's rest for everybody to recover from the excitement of the Great Fight.

As the brig now belonged to Peter and his band, having been taken in fair fight, they all put on Pirate clothes and started getting their vessel ready to sail. Peter, of course, became captain: who else could be? Tootles was bo'sun; Nibs and John were mate and second mate. The rest were plain A.B.s.

Some of the crew wanted to keep the *Jolly Roger* a pirate craft: some, again, thought honesty was the best policy. What Peter intended, nobody knew, and nobody dared ask: for he was not only wearing

Hook's suits (altered by Wendy to fit him), but putting on a very good imitation of Hook's manner: hooking his forefinger to look like a claw, and sticking the two-cigar holder in his mouth.

He gave orders to head the ship for the Azores: once there, it would be quicker to fly the rest of the way. It was therefore supposed by the crew that Peter was taking the little Darlings home again. But no such plans were in his head. He was growing as cunning as Hook himself.

Meanwhile, all this time Mr and Mrs Darling were hopefully and hopelessly expecting their children's return. I mean, sometimes they hoped like anything, and other times they hadn't a ha'porth of hope left. They kept the three little beds aired, and the nursery window open: Mrs Darling never left the house. Everything was ready to welcome the wanderers, and everything was just the same as it had always been, except that the kennel was absent from the nursery between nine and six.

This was because, after the children's flight, Mr Darling took all the blame on himself, for having chained up Nana in the yard. He said Nana was far wiser than he, and that they had better change places. So he crawled into the kennel, and vowed that he would never leave it until his children came home again. Every morning he was taken in a cab (still in the kennel) to his office; every evening he was brought back the same way. And in the kennel he stayed as long as he was up. He could not take it into bed with him: there wasn't room; but he went to parties in it, and became extremely popular. As for his courtesy to Nana, it was almost painful.

But they each felt that what had happened was due to their own faults. Mrs Darling would say, 'If only I had not accepted that invitation to dinner at No. 27!' Mr Darling would say, 'If only I had not been so fidgety and cross with Nana!' And Nana would moan, 'If only they had not had a dog, like me, for a nurse!'

One evening Mr Darling came home in the kennel, surrounded by a cheering crowd. He was rather enjoying his punishment: it had made him such a celebrated person. Mrs Darling and Nana, who had not borne their punishment in public, sat mournfully in the night-nursery by the open window. But presently Mrs Darling went into the day-nursery and played 'Home, Sweet Home,' on the piano, so tenderly that Mr Darling curled up and fell asleep in the kennel.

Suddenly two people entered at the window – Peter and Tinker Bell. They closed and barred the window, so that Wendy might think her mother had shut her out, and go back to the Island with Peter. This sly and Hookish plan had been in his head ever since he took command of the ship.

But Peter was not so heartless as he made out: and when he saw Mrs Darling, who was very pretty, shedding tears (and he knew that was because of Wendy), he unbarred the window again, and flung it wide. 'Come along, Tink!' he said, 'we don't want any silly blubbing mothers.' And away they went. Not very far, though.

Directly after, Wendy, John, and Michael flew in. They were disappointed at finding Mr Darling asleep in the kennel instead of Nana. Still more disappointed, that their mother was not standing waiting to welcome them. But when they heard her playing in the next room, they knew she would come in shortly. Each child slipped into its own bed.

Mrs Darling soon returned to the night-nursery: and there were the three little heads in the three little beds, just as she had so often dreamed she saw them. She thought she was dreaming still, and sat down sadly by the fire. Then they all jumped out and ran into her arms. Oh! how utterly lovely! 'Oh, Mummy!' – 'Oh, my sweet dears!'

And Mr Darling awoke, and Nana hurried in, and everybody was unbelievably happy – except Peter, who stared in at the window, and wondered what it felt like to have a real mother, after all. He was not exactly envious, but he was a wee bit less cocky than usual, and snubbed Tink when she wanted him to be off.

How long had the children been away? That I cannot tell you. You see, they did not bother about dates and months: and there was only the Crocodile-time to tell them hours. But it was not so short, perhaps, as it seemed to them: and not so long as it seemed to Mrs Darling.

The other boys waited downstairs, until they thought the surprises and explanations would be over. They counted up to five hundred: then they walked upstairs, and stood in a row before Mrs Darling. They had taken their hats off, but were awkward in their Pirate clothes. Mrs Darling was quite willing, as Wendy had promised, to adopt them: but Mr Darling thought six extra boys rather a lot. However, by careful arrangement of the drawing-room furniture,

corners were found for all the boys, without having to enlarge No. 14.

Mrs Darling also offered to adopt Peter, who would only converse through the window. But when he learned that he would be sent to school, and probably to an office, and would be a man before long, he declined – rather roughly. He was so horribly afraid of being caught and made into a grown-up, and perhaps even having a beard.

'I shall live with Tink,' said he, 'in the little house we built for Wendy. The fairies are fixing it high up beside their nests in the treetops.'

'How lovely!' cried Wendy longingly. 'But you will be so lonely in the evenings.'

'Well, can't you come back with me?'

'May I, mother? Just for a short time.'

'Certainly not,' said Mrs Darling. But Peter looked so downcast, that she very nobly offered to let Wendy go for a week every year to the little house, to do Peter's spring-cleaning. This having been settled, Peter flew away quite gaily.

At the end of the first year, he came back to fetch Wendy. She was now the only one who could fly. John and Michael had entirely lost their flying-power as time went on. They had to go to school, and then they blamed Wendy bitterly for not letting them stay on the Island. Later on, they grew so accustomed to things, that they became quite commonplace, ordinary little boys, and entirely forgot their wonderful life in the Neverland.

But they were not the only forgetful ones. For, when Wendy was talking over old times with Peter, up in the little house in the treetops, she found that his mind was a blank about bygone adventures. He had enjoyed so many new ones in the course of the year. He even asked, 'Who is Captain Hook?' And on being reminded how he had killed Hook and saved the lives of all the children, Peter seemed scarcely interested. 'I forget people,' he said, 'after I have killed them.'

Presently, Tinker Bell being mentioned, he actually enquired, 'Who is Tinker Bell?' He could not remember, even after Wendy had explained. He said, 'There are such a lot of fairies about.'

Wendy was rather shocked. It looked as if the time would come when Peter would say carelessly, 'Who is Wendy?' But she did a great spring-cleaning for him, all the same. 'If *he* forgets,' she told herself, 'anyhow I never can.'

Next year he did not come to fetch her. Wendy, grieved and hurt, waited in vain. But the third year he arrived: and did not seem to know that he had missed last time. Certainly his memory was getting worse and worse. However, Wendy did not find fault with him. She spring-cleaned again: and it was sweet to sit with Peter in the little house of an evening, after the day's work was done.

And that was the end of Wendy's visits to the Neverland. For, after this, years and years and years went by, without a sign of Peter. The boys all grew up: Michael became an engine-driver, and Tootles a judge, and Slightly a lord, and so on. Wendy not only grew up, but married and had a daughter named Jane. Who could have believed it?

Mrs Darling was dead: Nana was dead; Mr Darling could not have squeezed into the kennel to save his life. There were only two people sleeping in the night-nursery – Jane and her nurse. Sometimes Wendy put Jane to bed, and then she would tell her long, long stories about Peter Pan. It was difficult to make Jane understand that Wendy could not fly any longer. She loved to listen to the tales about the fairies, the Pirates, the Redskins, the Mermaids, the home under the ground, and the little house. By and by, she had heard these adventures so often, she knew about them better than her mother.

'What was the last thing Peter ever said to you?' Jane asked, one evening.

'He said, "You'll always be waiting for me, and then some night you will hear me crowing."'

'What was his crow like?'

'Like this' – and Wendy tried to imitate it.

But Jane replied gravely, 'No, it wasn't. It was like this.' And she did a much more life-like crow.

'My darling child, how in the world do you know?'

'Oh, I often hear it when I am asleep.'

This not only startled Wendy, but made her rather nervous, because Jane was her only child. She took to sitting in the nursery nearly every night, so as to keep an eye on Jane. And one night, as she was darning socks by firelight—

The window blew open, and Peter dropped in. Just as of old. He had not changed at all: and at first he did not notice that Wendy was now a big woman. 'Hullo, Wendy!' he said, as if he had seen her that afternoon. 'Hullo, Peter,' she replied, hoping he would not stay long; lest Jane should wake.

'Have you forgotten,' he asked rather severely, 'that this is spring-cleaning time?' It was no use to tell him that he had forgotten some fourteen or fifteen spring-cleaning times.

'I can't come,' said Wendy. 'I have forgotten how to fly. You can see for yourself.' And she turned up the light. Peter saw a tall, beautiful woman, and he gave a cry of pain. 'O Wendy! You promised not to grow up!'

'I couldn't help it, Peter. I grew up several years ago. I am married now.'

'No, you're not.'

'And that little girl in bed is my baby.'

'She's not!' cried Peter – and he moved towards Jane with his dagger lifted. But instead of stabbing her, he sat down on the floor, and sobbed in the most heartbroken manner. Wendy was so distressed that she left the room. She had no notion how to comfort him: and she hated to see him suffer.

Presently Peter's weeping wakened Jane. And she sat up in bed.

'Little boy, why are you crying?' He bowed to her, and she bowed to him – just as Wendy had done of old.

'My name is Peter Pan,' he remarked.

'Yes, I know,' said Jane. 'I was expecting you.'

When Wendy returned, with some cake for Peter, she found him sitting crowing on the bedpost, and Jane flying round the room in her nightie. It was a sight to freeze a loving mother. But Jane was having a perfectly splendid time.

Peter bid a hasty 'Goodbye' to Wendy, and was just floating through the window with Jane, when Wendy caught hold of her child, crying 'No, no!'

'I'm only going for spring-cleaning time,' said Jane, 'he wants me always to do his spring-cleaning. And he does so need a mother. You see, Mummy, you can't fly.'

She had to let them fly away together. It was bound to happen sooner or later. She had always feared that it would.

But now Jane is herself a grown-up who can't fly, so she cannot boast over Wendy. And she has a small daughter called Margaret, whom Peter fetches away to the Neverland, every spring-cleaning time (unless

he forgets). Margaret tells him stories, mostly about himself, which she has heard from her mother and her grandmother. They all sound quite new to Peter; and, my goodness, doesn't he enjoy them! Especially those about himself.

Very likely Margaret will grow up and have a daughter who will go and mother Peter; and so on and so on, as far as can be seen. But, after all, first come is first served. The happiest days of all were those long-ago days, in the little house, with its two inhabitants – just Peter Pan and Wendy.

Peter Pan and Great Ormond Street Hospital for Children

Peter Pan, or the Boy who Would Not Grow Up, has been helping other children to grow up for almost 100 years.

The first performance of *Peter Pan* took place on 27 December 1904 at the Duke of York's Theatre in London to tremendous acclaim, and it was then published as a novel in 1911 by Hodder & Stoughton (now Hachette Children's Books). Over 100 years later, Peter Pan, Tinker Bell, Captain Hook and all their friends are still enchanting children and adults alike.

In April 1929, J M Barrie left the rights to *Peter Pan* to Great Ormond Street Hospital for Children and this provision was confirmed in his Will at his death in 1937. This meant that whenever the play or one of its many adaptations is staged, or whenever a copy of *Peter Pan* is bought, the Hospital will benefit. Though childless himself, Barrie loved children and had long been a supporter of the hospital, and his exceptional gift was a natural expression of that support. His wish that the amount of money raised should never be revealed has always been respected by the Hospital.

The benefits from this most generous gift are visible to every visitor to the Hospital and Peter Pan and J M Barrie are commemorated in many wards and departments of Great Ormond Street Hospital.

Registered Charity No. 235825 © 1989 2006 GOSHCC